A GOLDEN TICKET MEANT FOR ME

by

Nicole Dawn Cottrell

Stories
From
Nicole's
Pen

A Golden Ticket Meant For Me

Copyright 2025, Nicole Dawn Cottrell

ISBN: 979-8-9937405-0-8

Book cover design and interior layout provided by
Self Publish Me Publishing Consulting and Book Design
Services for Independent Authors.
www.selfpublishme.com | email: info@selfpublishme.com

This book is lovingly dedicated to my
grandmother, Katherine Carter, and my Aunt Tommie
Cottrell. Thank you both for your love, your wisdom,
and your guidance. I carry your words, your strength,
and your spirit with me every single day.

A GOLDEN TICKET MEANT FOR ME

Chapter 1:
The Fabulous Four Reunite

The last time the four of us had been together, life had felt like one big open door. Now, five years later, Chyna, Alexis, Morgan, and I were finally meeting up for brunch. It was a warm Saturday afternoon in Las Vegas, the kind of dry heat you forget about until it wraps around you the moment you step outside. The reunion felt long overdue. Back in high school we had been thick as thieves, inseparable until life, love, and responsibility pulled us in different directions.

We picked a chic spot in Summerlin, a swanky café known for its bottomless mimosas, truffle fries, and honey-lavender chicken and waffles that kept people lined up outside every weekend.

The moment we saw each other, we screamed and folded into one another like no time had passed at all. Chyna was still the rebel, tilting her head with that familiar smirk as she pushed her hair back and rocked her signature leather jacket despite the desert heat. Morgan, the fashionista, looked like she had walked straight out of a resort magazine, adjusting her sunglasses just so while her flowy sundress caught the breeze. Alexis click-clacked in like she was late to her own press conference, heels sharp, phone in one hand, iced latte in the other.

And me? I looked like a woman who had lived a lot of life in five years, carrying more than I was ready to confess. But I showed up. And right then, that felt like a small victory.

As we picked over charcuterie and sipped our second round of drinks, Alexis lit up with an idea. She waved her phone like a magic wand.

"Ladies, I have a plug. A private guided tour of the caverns in Arizona. Limousine pickup, champagne, the works. My travel agent still owes me for that Cabo disaster.

Who's in?"

She didn't wait. She called her contact right there at the table, speaker on full blast while the rest of us exchanged wide-eyed looks. The moment she hung up, the whole table lit up. Chyna tapped her ring against her glass in excitement. Morgan lifted her phone and snapped a quick video for her Instagram story. I covered my mouth to hide a laugh that felt good down to my soul. "Alright, ladies, next Saturday," Alexis announced. "Pick up is at nine. Be ready. And of course I'll have the champagne waiting."

We each sent Alexis the money through Apple Pay. Then we raised our glasses for a toast.

"To freedom," Chyna said.
"To new memories," Morgan added.
"To not letting life drain us dry," Alexis chimed in.

And me? I lifted my glass and whispered, "To finding myself again."

Four friends. One plan. And for the first time in a

long time, I felt like something good might finally be on its way.

Right then, the mood shifted from emotional to downright silly. That's when the reminiscing started. It began with Chyna cackling mid-bite. "Remember when we skipped school and went to that random house party in Henderson?"

Morgan nearly spit out her drink. "You mean the one where Alexis pretended to be a foreign exchange student from London?"

"Oh my God, yes!" Morgan said, laughing. "You kept that fake British accent up the whole night!"

Alexis smirked and slipped right back into character, lifting her pinky and saying in a crisp accent, "'Ello, I'm Ariana Kensington. Just transferred from boarding school just outside of London. My da's in the foreign ministry.'"

Morgan wiped away tears. "You told that poor boy you were related to Prince Harry!"

Chyna jumped in. "And that your favorite subject

was European tea culture. I couldn't even look at you without laughing."

"I gave him the number to the school library," Alexis added proudly. "He tried to call me the next day and got Ms. Jacobs, who nearly called the cops thinking it was a prank."

The stories kept rolling.

Like when Chyna got caught selling mini liquor bottles out of her locker and had the nerve to tell the assistant principal that it was Mr. Moore, the janitor, who was hiding the liquor there. "You know he had a drinking problem," Alexis claimed, "almost getting that poor man fired." The assistant principal was skeptical, but Chyna's audacity left everyone speechless. Mr. Moore was eventually cleared, but he never looked at us the same way again.

Or when Morgan convinced the substitute teacher she was the teacher's assistant and gave them hall passes like she ran the place, just so they could walk to McDonald's, tear up some fries, and flirt with the fine boys on the football team.

Then there was the infamous blunt-smoking session in the janitor's closet that nearly got them suspended. They talked their way out of it by blaming it on a Jamaican student who had just transferred in, claiming he didn't understand the school rules. The administration, not knowing him yet, actually believed it, and the girls walked away with nothing more than a warning.

"Oh! And remember the great escape of junior year?" Morgan said with a grin, giving Alexis a nudge. "When your mother finally fell asleep during your birthday sleepover, and we crept out to meet those Benz boys at the park?"

Everyone cracked up. Except me.

I stirred my lemonade and laughed. "Y'all know I wasn't part of that," I said. "My daddy would've materialized out of thin air like a genie, wearing one of those ribbed white undershirts folks call wife beaters, church socks and all, Bible in one hand and belt in the other, hollering 'the devil is a lie' while dragging me home." They howled. They knew. I was the sheltered one, growing up in a strict two-parent household with two sisters and a brother, watched over by a father who guarded us girls like we were on death row. While they were sneaking out windows, I was memorizing Bible verses. While they kissed boys under the bleachers, I was rehearsing for choir competitions.

"I didn't even wear lipstick until college, and while y'all were passing around vodka in soda bottles, I was worried about getting grounded for forgetting to sweep the porch," I reminded them.

Still, they made me feel like I belonged. They always had. Plus, deep down, I never had the desire to do all the bad and wild things they did.

We lingered at that café for hours, bellies full, cheeks sore from laughing. As we stood to leave, Alexis called out, "Nine a.m. sharp next Saturday, ladies. Don't make me send out a search party for y'all!"

We hugged long and tight, as if the warmth

between us could return us to the ease and closeness we had always shared.

Chapter 2:
Rolling in Style

◇

That whole week felt different after our brunch. Something in me shifted. Maybe it was nostalgia. Maybe it was the feeling of finally being seen again, not just as someone's ex-wife, someone's mom, or somebody's employee, but as Andi, the girl who had always played it safe.

Since my divorce a year ago, life has felt like one long emergency. My ex hasn't paid a dime of child support. Every dollar has to stretch, every dinner is built around coupons, and every utility bill feels like a prayer. I am tired down to my bones and feel alone more often than I'd ever admit. I'm keeping things together for my two kids with nothing more than willpower and the strength God gives me.

But that brunch with my girls lit something in me: hope, joy, and laughter, all the things I'd buried under stress and survival.

By Friday night, I had filled my purse with all the essentials for the caverns tour and found myself actually looking forward to the next morning. I stood in front of the mirror, adjusting my nightgown and ensuring everything was in order. The tiredness showed in my eyes, but my smile told a different story. I wasn't just a mother, a divorcée, or a woman burdened by life's hardships. I was Andi, a fighter, standing on the front lines, determined to hold it all together and carve out a place of peace for me and my children.

The next day, right on schedule, the limo pulled up in front of my house around fifteen after nine. The tinted windows gleamed in the morning sun, and when the driver stepped out in his sleek black suit to open the door, I could already hear laughter spilling out. Alexis was on FaceTime, talking to Morgan and Chyna at the same time.

Alexis had promised she would go all out, and as

usual, she didn't disappoint. Champagne nestled in a silver chiller, sweating slightly from the ice sitting at the center of a polished bar console. Crystal flutes gleamed like jewels, and there were silver trays lined with gourmet snacks: prosciutto-wrapped melon, smoked gouda cubes, caviar on toast points, and chocolate-dipped strawberries.

Alexis was the first one picked up, and true to form, she looked like a walking Vogue editorial. Silk blouse shining, oversized shades, gold heels, and a bag that screamed money. I was the second pick-up, and the moment I stepped in, she had already poured my flute of orange juice. She clinked her glass against mine with a smile. "To Andi," she said. "Let the fun begin."

Next came Chyna, loud and lively as always, strutting out of her front door like she was arriving on the red carpet. Her heels clicked with authority, and she wore a figure-hugging red jumpsuit, bangles stacked halfway up her arms, and her curly hair was pinned up with jeweled clips that sparkled every time she turned her head.

Morgan, always the edgy one, was last. She emerged in towering black stilettos, a leather mini, and a cropped designer jacket that would definitely turn heads. Her oversized sunglasses and crimson lipstick completed the look.

The three of them looked like they were headed to a movie premiere, while I, dressed in my jeans, tennis shoes, and a light pullover, looked like I was about to hike Mount Rainer.

But I didn't care. I had done my research. We were going into caves, dusty and damp, and I wasn't about to twist an ankle for the sake of fashion. Still, I couldn't help but laugh at how dramatically different we all looked, each of us dressed like we were headed to a completely different event.

The laughter settled into something warm and familiar as we drifted into reminiscing, giggling over memories from high school. We laughed about the time Morgan got suspended for pocketing money from the school concession stand, and the time Chyna tripped at prom and blamed it on Mr. Moore and his janitor's mop, insisting he had done it on purpose to get revenge for her blaming him for the liquor in her locker.

The thing is, she was right. I saw Mr. Moore walking away afterward, snickering to himself like he had just pulled off the crime of the century.

We were already a ways down the road, still laughing about it, when the drive settled into a blur of music, memories, and half-remembered stories. We sang along to old R&B hits, passed around gourmet snacks, and relived the wildest nights like no time had passed at all.

But then, about fifteen minutes from our destination, the limo driver's voice came over the intercom. "Ladies, just a heads-up, I'm passing your tour tickets back now."

He handed them over his shoulder, and Alexis began distributing them. "Ooooh, look at this! Our names are printed on them!" she said, handing one to each of us like she was dealing cards at a casino.

When mine landed in my lap, something immediately felt off.

Their tickets were glossy red, The Caverns of Hades Hollow Tour written in bright silver script. But the moment I looked down at mine, my stomach flipped. It wasn't red. It wasn't even close. My ticket shimmered gold, almost glowing in the sunlight. And where theirs showed the tour we booked, mine carried just four words: THE CELESTIAL CITY TOUR.

Chapter 3:
Celestial City

I lifted my ticket and squinted at it. "Wait a second... y'all, mine's different. Look."

The laughter died down as they peered at my ticket. "Uh-oh," Alexis said, frowning. "What in the world?" She asked the driver how this could be corrected, her tone shifting into the authoritative cadence she used during business meetings.

The driver's voice came through again, calm but apologetic: "Unfortunately, ma'am, the customer service office is closed on weekends. We can issue a refund on Monday, but I'm afraid we can't correct the tickets today."

I felt my stomach sink. The excitement that had

carried me through the morning suddenly deflated. I leaned back in my seat with a heavy sigh. A few hours from home, and somehow stuck with a different ticket? Of course this would happen to me.

The other girls immediately chimed in, trying to soothe the moment. "We can cancel," Chyna offered. "Seriously, it's no big deal. We'll go back home or find something else to do."

"No," I interrupted, shaking my head. "We've come all this way.
You all were so excited about this.
Please. Please.
Go enjoy it."

"But you'll be all alone," Morgan said quietly. "That's not right."

"I'll be fine," managing to form a small smile. "I'll just take some pictures and meet y'all after the tour."
The limo began to slow, and the driver spoke again. "Ladies, we've arrived at The Caverns of Hades

Hollow. Please be sure to take all your belongings."

The door swung open, and sunlight poured in. One by one, each of them paused before stepping out of the limo to hug me tightly. Their faces were full of worry and guilt.

"You sure?" Alexis asked for the third time, her hand resting on the door.

"Go," I nodded. "I'll be alright."

Once the door shut and they disappeared toward the entrance, the limo was quiet. Too quiet. I sat back with a heavy heart, watching the trees blur past the window as we started moving again. That's when the driver rolled down the divider and glanced at me through the rearview mirror.

"Ma'am," he began gently, "I know this mix-up feels like a disappointment right now. But I promise you, the Celestial City Tour is something very special. It's not a mistake. I've heard stories from folks who've taken that tour, and none of them came back the same."

His words sent a curious shiver down my spine.

"Not the same?"

He nodded solemnly.
"They say the tour is eye-opening. It shows you things you didn't even know you needed to see or understand. Sometimes, ma'am, what appears as a mistake can lead you right where you're meant to be."

I didn't know what to say. I stared at the golden ticket in my hand. It felt warm to the touch, like it had a heartbeat of its own.

After driving for a while and eventually turning onto Paradise Blvd, I felt the strangest sensation settle over me. It felt like fate had quietly taken over, guiding me toward something I didn't yet understand but knew I had to surrender to.

The driver's voice gently cut through the quiet hum of the road, calm and clear over the intercom.

"Ma'am, we'll be arriving at your destination in just a few minutes. Please be sure to gather all of your belongings."

Those words stirred something inside me. That nervous flutter I thought I'd tucked away began to rise again, swelling in my stomach and tightening in my chest. My heart thudded harder, each beat echoing the growing uncertainty in my mind. This wasn't just some casual sightseeing trip; I was stepping into the unknown and doing it alone.

I gathered my things slowly, fingers fumbling just a little. My jacket, my water bottle, my bag, all clutched tightly to me like a child holding its security blanket.

As the limo eased to a stop, the tires made a soft crunching sound beneath us, like we were arriving somewhere sacred, somewhere set apart from the rest of the world.

A moment later, the driver stepped out and came around the vehicle. With smooth, deliberate grace, he opened the door and offered me his hand. I stepped out into the sunlight, blinking against the light as I adjusted to the world outside.

The air felt different here, lighter somehow, like it had shed the weight of the ordinary.

The driver studied my face with a gentle intensity, his eyes seeing more than I wanted to admit. He placed a steady hand on my shoulder, "Ma'am," he said softly, his voice wrapped in warmth and certainty, "there's no need to be scared. You don't have to carry that nervousness any further. This is more than just a tour. It's an experience that was meant for you. You're going to be just fine. Better than fine."

Something in his tone, in the way he looked at me, not with pity, but with calm assurance, started to undo the knot of fear in my stomach. My breath came easier. The stiffness in my posture melted away. A flicker of confidence returned, enough for a small, genuine smile to lift the corners of my mouth.

Then he turned and pointed just ahead.
"There," he said, nodding toward a glimmering sight in the near distance, "you see that bridge?"

I followed his gaze, and there it was.

A stunning wooden arch bridge, painted white and trimmed with intricate carvings, stretched gracefully over a sparkling creek. But it wasn't just the craftsmanship that caught my breath. The bridge shimmered, literally shimmered, as if dusted in stardust. Light bounced off its surface in waves, casting tiny rainbows in the air and making the whole structure look like something out of a dream. It was glowing, almost humming with magic, like it had been waiting for me all along.

"That's the way," the driver said with a knowing smile. "Just walk across the bridge, and you'll find the entrance to Celestial City."

Still spellbound by the beauty before me, I turned back to him with a deeper smile and a heart full of gratitude. I didn't say a word. I didn't need to. He gave me a slight nod in return, his eyes twinkling as if he understood everything I was feeling.

And so, I walked. One step at a time, toward that radiant bridge. Each footfall was steady, guided by something greater than me. As I reached the start of the arch, the sunlight seemed to bend and dance around me, as if the universe itself was cheering me on.

I took one last glance over my shoulder. He was still there, watching with a calm smile, arms folded, nodding slowly.

Then I turned back toward the light and began crossing the bridge into something that felt entirely new and entirely mine.

Chapter 4:
The Golden Ticket

———— ◇ ————

As I paused at the crest of the bridge, looking down, something extraordinary unfolded before me, something I could never have imagined, even in my wildest dreams.

The air shimmered with a golden haze, and suddenly, the world on the other side of that arch exploded into a spectrum of colors so vivid, so unearthly, that my breath caught in my throat.

These weren't ordinary colors. No, they weren't just brighter. They were otherworldly. They pulsed and danced with a life of their own, hues shifting like waves of emotion. Radiant violets streaked with liquid starlight, blues deeper than any ocean I had ever seen, and soft, glowing greens that seemed to hum with peace. Some colors defied all names or comparisons, shimmering in hues that felt imagined rather than real, as if I had wandered into a realm far beyond the reach of my earthly senses.

As I continued to walk a little further along the bridge, I paused mid-step and looked down. The planks beneath me glowed softly, alive with flowing hues that moved like liquid light. Gentle waves of color bent and swirled with each step, as though the bridge itself were welcoming me.

Then, without warning, a voice boomed through the air. Deep and resonant, it came from every direction at once, vibrating through my chest like a drumbeat. The only comparison I could make to this experience was that scene in The Wizard of Oz when the Wizard's voice surrounded Dorothy and her friends. But this felt different. This felt personal, as if the voice knew me and had been waiting for me.

"Welcome," the voice declared, powerful, tender, and inviting. "This place is everything you've ever dreamed of, and so much more."

I gasped, not from fear, but from the overwhelming wonder that swept through me. My heart pounded with anticipation as the bridge gently ended and I stepped onto solid ground again.

Before me stood a grand arched gateway, carved from a substance that shimmered like crystal and the brightest of stars. It gleamed under the golden light.

Standing beneath the arch was a ticket taker with a radiant smile and knowing eyes. But he wasn't dressed in flowing robes or elaborate garments. No, he wore simple clothes: a clean white button-down shirt with the sleeves rolled up, well-worn jeans, and sneakers. He looked like someone you might pass on the street and never think twice about, yet his presence radiated calm and peacefulness.

As I stood there, still in awe of this incredible place, I realized I wasn't alone. When I glanced around, I saw others nearby, each holding a ticket, their faces filled with the same wonder and awe I felt. We had all arrived together, yet somehow it still felt like this moment had been created just for me.

Without a word, I handed him the golden ticket I'd been holding. Its surface now seemed to come to life somehow, glowing faintly with a soft light. He accepted it with a quiet nod and, in return, handed me something that looked like a map, though calling it a map hardly did it any justice. It felt alive in my hands.

The parchment unfurled itself gently, revealing glowing paths, pulsating destinations, and shifting corridors that moved as I looked at them. It seemed to respond to my curiosity, adjusting itself to reflect the places I wanted to explore. Light flickered across its surface like ripples on water, guiding my gaze toward the path ahead. I then clutched it tightly as I stepped forward through the gateway.

Beneath my feet, the ground transformed. It became an iridescent trail of gold, warm like sunlight and as smooth as polished glass, yet it yielded gently beneath me with each step. The path glowed faintly with every movement, pulsing softly in response as though it recognized my presence. It stretched forward, winding through the landscape like a living current, quietly beckoning me deeper into this strange and glorious realm.

The others who had arrived with me, crossing the same bridge just moments before, exchanged glances as we took it all in. Some smiled shyly, while others remained suspended in the same spellbound trance I was still experiencing. Though no words were spoken, there was an instant connection between us, a quiet understanding that we were all part of something much larger than ourselves.

There was no fear here. No sense of competition, urgency, or confusion. Only a profound stillness wrapped in wonder, love, and quiet gratitude. It felt like every soul present understood, without needing to speak, that we had been invited into something sacred, something rare, something far greater than ourselves.

I felt light on my feet, nearly weightless, like a child at the gates of Disney World for the very first time, only amplified a thousandfold. This wasn't just joy. It was euphoria unlike anything I had ever known. It surged through me like a wave of golden light, flooding every corner of my being. A warmth bloomed in my chest, expanding until it felt like my heart might burst.

My skin tingled. My chest lifted. I had never felt this alive in my lifetime. And just as the feeling settled into every inch of me, the world around me seemed to open wider.

The glowing path stretched before me, lined with arched corridors and mysterious entryways visible in the distance. Some shimmered like glass. Others were carved into hillsides or tucked behind cascading vines. Each one whispered of something different: adventure, healing, discovery, memory.

And so, holding my enchanted map close, with my heart pounding and eyes wide with wonder, I smiled and stepped forward.

Chapter 5:
The Tomato Grove

———————— ◇ ————————

Each step felt like it carried me deeper into a realm untouched by earthly hands. The ground beneath me shimmered with a quiet energy, pulsing gently under my feet like a heartbeat, one that I found myself slowly falling in sync with.

I walked slowly, deliberately, unable to rush. Not just because the moment demanded reverence, but because every detail seemed to shift and shimmer as I moved, as if this realm was actively revealing itself one breathtaking moment at a time.

Then, something caught my eye to the right. At first, I thought I was simply passing a grove of trees, tall and elegant, their branches swaying gently in the golden breeze. But as I turned my head, my footsteps slowed to a halt. A warm rush swept through my chest. I stared, eyes wide, mouth slightly parted.

These were no ordinary trees. Their trunks were sleek and smooth, with bark that shimmered like it had been brushed with crushed pearls and glowing dew. Veins of silver ran up their sides like streams of early dawn's light flowing through the wood.

Their leaves, oh, the leaves, fluttered with such lightness, glowing blazingly, as though kissed by the sun and the moon at once.

I instantly noticed the grass beneath my feet. It was unbelievably soft, velvety and warm, softer than clouds in a dream. Yet even that small miracle vanished from my mind when I looked up.

It was the fruit that truly arrested me. Hanging from the branches were numerous fruit shapes that glimmered unlike anything from the world I knew. They weren't shaped like apples or pears or anything I recognized. Some looked iridescent, like teardrops made of glass, while others glowed like tiny suns suspended by delicate stems. Some were smooth, shimmering in opalescent blues and radiant pinks. Others were textured with speckled-skin color variations, their hues shifting as I stared, as if the fruit could decide what it wanted to become.

And the longer I looked, the more the trees revealed, as if the trees were gradually allowing me to witness what they truly held.

There were shades I had no name for, colors that didn't exist in any crayon box or artist's palette. One piece of fruit shimmered in a shade somewhere between gold and lavender, constantly shifting depending on how the light struck it. Another glowed a pale, transparent teal that looked like it held a miniature galaxy within.

Then I leaned in, squinting, certain I saw what looked like tiny constellations swirling inside the skin of the fruit. It was mesmerizing. I reached out instinctively, my fingers trembling as they hovered

36

just inches from one of the glowing fruits, but I paused. Not out of fear, but awe. It felt sacred, like everything in this place had meaning and purpose.

As I stood there, suspended in that moment of reverence, a gentle breeze stirred the air around me. The scent from the trees drifted in, delicate and unfamiliar. Sweet like honey, but lighter, mingled with the crispness of fresh rainfall and a floral note I couldn't quite place. It wrapped around me like a memory just out of reach, comforting and soothing. The fragrance stirred something in me, something deeper than memory. It felt like a truth my soul remembered, even if my mind did not.

Drawn forward by that feeling, I continued walking, the path leading me deeper into wonder. Each tree I passed revealed something new. Some bore clusters of luminous fruit that hung low enough to brush the tops of the grassland, while others stood majestic and proud, their branches stretching toward the glowing sky as their fruit dangled like glowing lanterns in a dream.

Slowly, I turned my gaze back to the path, though I couldn't help stealing one last look at the trees. A quiet thought rose inside me: What if the fruit wasn't just meant to be seen, but chosen?

The idea sat with me, deep and stirring, but I kept walking. I wasn't ready to pick one. Nooo... not yet. Not until I understood more.

Still, I carried that image with me, my heart steady with wonder, my senses stretched wide to whatever this realm wanted to show me next.

So, when the path opened into the first corridor, I was immediately swept into another setting.

At first, I noticed the sunlight, warmer here than it had been on the footpath. It poured in through a glowing sky that seemed to stretch forever, casting everything in a soft, golden hue.

But what truly caught my attention were the rows and rows of tomato plants, stretching as far as my eyes could see, blanketing the land like a crimson sea.

Only, they weren't just tomato plants. These were towering giants. Their vines weren't wrapped around stakes or poles like in the gardens back home. No, these vines had grown so enormous they resembled tree trunks, some rising ten, maybe even twenty feet into the air. The huge vines spiraled upward, heavy with fruit, like living chandeliers of ripening red jewels.

It wasn't a tomato field. It was a tomato forest.

I stood there in awe, my mouth slightly open, trying to comprehend the scale of it all. The fruit glistened with dew, some of it glowing faintly, and the scent in the air was earthy and rich, like summer, soil, and something more ancient. Something sacred.

Then I noticed movement. Just ahead, maybe thirty or forty feet into the grove, stood two figures: a young woman and an older man. Both were dressed in overalls, their sleeves rolled up, boots caked in red clay. They looked like farmers, timeless and rooted. The woman had her hair tied back in a simple scarf, while the man wore a straw hat so old and worn it looked like it had seen a thousand harvests.

There was a rhythm to their movement, an unspoken language in how they worked. They were tending to the plants, loading trays of tomato starters into the bed of an old, faded light blue pickup truck. The truck looked like it had been plucked out of the 1950s. Its paint was chipped, the tires worn, yet somehow it seemed untouched by rust or time. In its bed were rows of baby tomato plants, their tiny leaves bright with promise.

Overcome with excitement, I stepped forward and spoke without hesitation.
"Hi there! This is incredible. I've never seen anything like this in my life. The tomatoes, the trees, they're amazing!"

They didn't look up. Didn't pause. Just kept working. I smiled awkwardly and tried again.
"Are you part of the harvest crew? Do others help harvest all of this? I mean, it must take an army to keep up with something this enormous."

Still, nothing.

They moved with a quiet grace, as if they were in a different rhythm, entirely. Their hands were gentle, almost reverent, as they touched the vines, plucked the ripest fruit, and arranged the plants in the truck with care. Their silence wasn't harsh. It was hollow. Empty, like a space I couldn't reach. A flicker of sadness suddenly passed over me. Their lack of response stung more than I expected, especially in a place that had felt so welcoming up until now. I had thought this corridor would at least offer some conversation. But they treated me like I wasn't even there.

Disheartened, I sighed and turned back toward the entrance, preparing to leave the way I had come. I had only taken a few steps when I heard her voice, clear and certain, cutting through the quiet breeze.

"Andi."

I stopped cold. My name. She had said my name.

I turned around slowly, pulse quickening. The woman farmer now stood alone near the entrance I had come through, with the man no longer in sight. Her hands were outstretched, and in them were two small tomato plants, each cradled like precious treasure.

"Take these," she said, her voice calm but firm. "Plant them as soon as you return home."

I blinked, caught between surprise and curiosity. "I... yes. Of course. Thank you."

I stepped forward, gently taking the plants from her hands. They were warm to the touch, and the roots buzzed with a strange, subtle energy, as if something inside them was still waking up. I looked down at the seedlings, then back up at her, but she had already turned away.

"I really appreciate this," I called out as I backed away toward the corridor's entrance. "Thank you, truly."

There was no reply. She continued walking back toward the massive vines, her posture strong, her silence intact.

Still holding the plants close to my chest, I turned

again to leave, but something very strange happened. A flicker of light passed over the grove behind me, almost like a ripple of lightning.

I glanced back over my shoulder and froze.

The faces of the two farmers, now both standing together once more, had changed. A faint purple hue had bloomed across their features, starting at their temples and slowly spreading across their skin like twilight settling over a landscape. It wasn't natural to me. It felt as though they were transforming into something foreign, strange and unfamiliar in a way that unsettled me instantly. A quick, rising fear surged within me, as if I had glimpsed something I was never meant to witness.

My breath caught in my throat. For a split second, I thought maybe I was imagining it, that the strangeness of this place was playing tricks on my mind. But no, it was real. The purple glow deepened, their expressions completely unchanged, as if this transformation was as normal to them as breathing.

I stood frozen, unsure whether to speak again or run. Fear finally broke my stillness. Clutching the two glowing plants tightly, I turned and hurried down the corridor as my heart pounded in my ears, and I didn't look back.

As I crossed the threshold out of the corridor and back onto the golden path, I had to stop and catch my breath. My heart still raced, and the image of their glowing, silent faces burned in my mind like a question without an answer.

Had I truly seen what I thought I saw? Why did this happen to me?

I looked down at the plants in my hands. Their leaves were still glowing, gently pulsing with a rhythm I could now feel in my palms. Well, whatever they were, they had been entrusted to me. And somehow, I knew they were important.

Chapter 6:
Design Your Home

As I continued to make my way away from the tomato grove, my heart, still stirred by what I had witnessed, slowly began to calm. The path ahead felt brighter now, lighter with each step. I tucked the plants gently into the crook of my arm and wandered forward, still dazed by what I had seen.

Soon, another archway appeared. This one was made of swirling vines and delicate blossoms. Above the archway floated the glowing words: DESIGN YOUR HOME.

Curious, I stepped through.

Immediately, the realm began to change around

me.

The ground beneath me was solid and dry, with a fine, grainy texture, like walking on warm sandstone. Above, the sky stretched endlessly, brilliant and vast.

As I stood there, a woman approached, and I recognized her immediately.

She was another tourist, someone I remembered seeing when we first entered the city. Like me, she had arrived wide-eyed and full of wonder, taking it all in for the first time.

Now, she caught my arm gently, her face lighting up with childlike excitement.

"Picture your dream home," she whispered. "And it will appear."

I blinked at her, surprised but somehow comforted by the small connection.
"My dream home?"

She nodded eagerly. "Anything you desire. Imagine

it. Feel it. And watch."

I hesitated.
Could it really be that simple?

Slowly, I closed my eyes and let my soul speak.

"This place responds to you," she said softly, her voice carrying the thrill of endless possibilities. "It's like it reads your soul and answers your dreams before you can even finish forming them."

I pictured it clearly now:

A breathtaking home, perched right at the edge of the water, just like those stunning homes tucked into the cliffs off the Puget Sound. Wide glass walls opening straight onto the Sound, blurring the line between indoors and nature. Soaring cedar beams stretched across vaulted ceilings. A vast library, its architecture, a harmonious blend of natural wood and timeless design. The walls were lined with floor-to-ceiling bookshelves, crafted from rich, warm-toned wood, each shelf brimming with my favorite books. A massive stone fireplace climbed two full stories high, anchoring the space with warmth and grandeur.

Outside, a wraparound deck hugged the house, with a firepit crackling in the corner and an infinity pool that looked as though it spilled directly into the endless blue beyond. The scent of honeysuckle lingered in the air as waves gently lapped against the shore and seagulls glided low across the water.

When I opened my eyes, it was there.

Standing proud and perfect before me, shimmering like it had been kissed by light.

Tears welled up in my eyes.

I stood there barefoot, feeling the warm earth beneath my feet, the sea breeze wrapping around me like a long-lost friend.

The woman gave me a small, knowing smile before she turned and drifted away, blending back into the crowd of other tourists.

It wasn't just any home.

It was my home.

The one my soul had always dreamed of but had never dared to believe could exist.

After soaking it all in, I finally turned toward the exit, following the path with a renewed sense of wonder, eager to discover what other miracles this beautiful place still held for me.

Chapter 7:
A Family Tied by Spirit

— ◇ —

As I approached another corridor, I noticed a subtle shift in the atmosphere. The air grew warmer, saltier, brushed with the familiar scent of the sea. Then came the unmistakable sound of ocean waves rolling against the shore, rhythmic and soothing, like a lullaby composed just for my soul.

My heart quickened. I've always had a deep connection to the sea. There's just something about the water. It speaks to me, whispers to places in my spirit I didn't even know existed.

Drawn forward by the sound, I stepped into the corridor and froze. A wave of stillness swept through me, anchoring me in place. Before me stretched the most beautiful shoreline I had ever laid eyes on.

Nooo... not just beautiful. It was enchanting.

The water glistened like liquid crystal, so clear I could see straight to the ocean floor. Coral gardens bloomed beneath the surface, and vibrant sea creatures swam effortlessly through their depths. But the most mesmerizing part? The water changed colors right before my eyes, shifting from sapphire blue to iridescent green, then melting into breathtaking shades of rose gold, soft blush, vivid magenta, and other hues I couldn't even name. It was like the ocean was painting emotions across the waves.

I felt a surge of childlike wonder. And without thinking, I kicked off my shoes and stepped onto the sand. It was warm and sooo...impossibly soft, like baby powder. It kissed the soles of my feet and trickled between my toes, making me laugh aloud from sheer joy.

I couldn't help myself. I laid down flat in the sand

and stretched my arms wide, moving them back and forth, making sand angels like I used to do in the snow as a child. I closed my eyes, letting the moment soak into every pore. I was completely consumed by peace, delight, and gratitude.

But then, I sensed a presence. A shadow passed gently over my face.

My eyes fluttered open. Standing above me was a striking woman in a flowing light blue dress that glowed with sacred brilliance. Her eyes held wisdom, her smile was soft yet knowing, and her energy pulsed with familiarity. She looked like someone I had always known but could never quite name.

"Are you enjoying yourself?" she asked, her voice melodic, like a song carried in the breeze.

Startled and slightly embarrassed by my childlike display, I scrambled to my feet, brushing the sand from my arms.

"Yes," I laughed nervously. "I suppose I got a little carried away."

52

She chuckled and offered her hand.

"I'm Jane," she said gently. "One of your paternal great-grandmothers, and one of the main ones assigned to watch over you."

Time stopped cold, like the world had exhaled and forgotten to breathe again.

"My great-grandmother?" I repeated, trying to catch up with the rush of emotion swelling inside me.

She nodded.

"I lived in the North, just before the Civil War. If you trace your lineage, you'll find me. My full name was Jane Polite."

I blinked.

"Polite? I've never heard that surname connected to my family," I said, heart pounding. "My maiden name was McGuire."

A smile tugged at the corner of her mouth. She was already aware of that, of course.

I began listing other family names that came down

my paternal line: Gill, Cooks, Demery. I searched her face for recognition.

She looked me directly in the eyes.

"You are a descendant of the Polite line," she said with unwavering certainty.

There was something in her gaze, something deeper than words. It was as if she was telling me more than she could say aloud. There was a knowing in her expression that both intrigued and unsettled me.

So, I asked the question I wasn't sure I wanted the answer to. "Am I biologically a McGuire?"

She tilted her head, a shadow crossing her eyes, and said softly,
"You can take a DNA test when you return home or just let sleeping dogs lie."

The words hit me like a wave. I stood there, stunned, my heart thudding in my chest. The possibility that my name, my history, might not be what I thought was almost too much to process. I was flabbergasted, caught between curiosity and confusion.

She stepped forward and embraced me, her arms as comforting as warm blankets on a cold night.

"It's time for me to go now," she whispered. "But in those moments when you feel like giving up, remember that you are strong, and I am always with you, helping you."

I held her tightly for a moment longer, reluctant to let go. Then, as she turned and walked away, something miraculous happened.

A soft wind stirred, and from the sky, a magnificent swarm of lavender-colored butterflies descended in a spiral, swirling above me like a living cloud. They began to shape themselves in midair, forming a perfect heart, as it glowed against the blue horizon.

And inside that heart appeared the face of my mother-in-law.

My breath caught in my throat. She had passed

away ten years ago, and not a day had gone by that I hadn't thought of her. We had shared something rare. Something sacred. A deep connection, as if we were kindred spirits who had been waiting lifetimes to find one another. We laughed together, shared our dreams, went on shopping trips and special lunch dates. Her loss had left a hole in me.

Seeing her now, framed in butterflies, brought tears instantly to my eyes.

Her voice drifted toward me like the soft rustle of leaves.

She greeted me just like she always did, with a warm, "How you doing?" Then she added, "I couldn't let you leave today without seeing you."

I clutched my chest.

"I miss you so much," I whispered, tears running freely now.

She smiled warmly.
"I would've come in person, but I'm on a very special assignment today, helping some children

who need guidance. I can't stay long, but I had to pop in and tell you that I love you. You're always in my heart. And yes, I visit you often. More than you know."

My lips trembled as I tried to respond, but all I could do was nod.

She seemed to understand, blowing me kiss after kiss, her beautiful face dimming gradually while butterflies spiraled upward, sweeping across the sky until they melted into the light.

I stood there, overwhelmed, speechless, surrounded by the warmth of love that reached beyond time, beyond space, beyond death itself.

And just like that, she was gone.

But her love remained, draping itself around me like a warm, everlasting hug.

Chapter 8:
A Table Set for Me

———— ◇ ————

Leaving the shoreline, with its shifting hues still fresh in my mind, I was jolted back to reality by a sudden, deep hunger. The urge was immediate and impossible to ignore.

So, I followed the path ahead, and soon the map revealed an entire district called The Celestial Commons, a dining area so beautifully designed it looked more like a sacred garden than a food court. The names of the eateries shimmered across the map like a divine menu: *Heavenly Bites & Buffet, Manna & More, Angel's Table, The Bread of Life Bistro, Peter's Pantry, and Wings & Things.*

Each one sounded more inviting than the last, but Heavenly Bites & Buffet called to me in a way I couldn't explain. Maybe it was the word "buffet," the promise of variety and abundance. Or maybe it was something deeper, perhaps something waiting for me there.

As I approached, the aroma reached me first, touching my soul before I even stepped inside. It wasn't just food. It was memory and emotion, seasoning and comfort, all wrapped in warmth. I stepped through the grand arched doorway into a space filled with soft golden light and a peace that settled deep inside me.

The buffet counter stretched before me, glowing beneath crystal fixtures that sparkled like scattered diamonds. Behind it stood a man with kind eyes and a gentle smile, greeting me as if he had known me forever.

"Hello, Andi. What would you like to have for lunch today?"

I paused.

"You know my name?"

He nodded. "Of course we do. We all know you

here. And everything you love has been prepared for you."

I stepped closer and glanced down the line, my heart tightening with emotion.

There it was: Salisbury steak, drenched in rich gravy, just the way I like it. Beef stroganoff, creamy and thick. Fried crappie, golden and crisp. Cabbage sautéed with just enough spice. And then, near the end, a dish that almost brought tears to my eyes: peach cobbler, warm and bubbling, cinnamon and buttery crust rising in waves.

Every dish was something I loved. Nothing altered. Nothing missing. And every bit of it was mine.

"I'll start with just a little of the first five entrees," I said, trying not to sound like a greedy child. My voice came out softer than I meant it to, with awe slipping through no matter how hard I tried to hold it back.

"You can return for more, as often as you like," the man said with a quiet certainty. "There's no shortage here."

I carried my tray to a table tucked beneath a golden vine that bloomed with glowing flowers.

I sat down and took my first bite, and froze. The flavor was more than delicious. It was sacred. Each dish tasted like it had been made with more than just skill. It was infused with love, care, and memory that pulled at my heart. It reminded me of the meals my grandmother used to make. She was an incredible cook, and somehow, this food brought her right back to me.

Eventually I lost track of time. Over and over again, I returned for more. I ate until I felt not just satisfied, but restored.

When I finally glanced at my watch, a flicker of urgency returned. Two hours had already passed, and I had only two more before the limo would arrive to pick me up. I still had so much left to see.

With a reluctant sigh, I gathered my things and stood. The warmth of the buffet clung to me like a blessing. But before leaving, I turned once more to glance back. The man behind the counter gave me a knowing nod, as if to say, Go on now. There's more waiting.

So, I did. I stepped out and returned to the main walking path, with the last bite of peach cobbler still warm on my tongue. But I wasn't ready to check the map again. Not yet. Something inside me stirred, a soft whisper inviting me to surrender and let the path reveal what came next.

With that urge, I moved forward, unburdened and open to whatever was in store for me next.

Chapter 9:
Rachel's Request

U p until now, every corridor I stepped into had felt like its own blessing, each one more awe-inspiring and soul-stirring than the last. A gentle breeze drifted at my back, nudging me forward, and the golden light along the trail seemed to brighten, almost as if it were urging me to keep going.

Then I saw it.

Nestled between two clusters of flowering trees stood an archway. It wasn't grand or glistening like some of the others. It was a simple white wooden frame with ivy trailing softly along its sides. Above it, in delicate gold script, the words shimmered: CORRIDOR OF REUNION.

The words alone caused my breath to stall. My feet hesitated, heart pounding, not out of fear, but anticipation. I stepped beneath the arch and was immediately greeted by the sight of a white picket fence that stretched across a rolling field. It looked like the countryside, familiar and comforting. The kind of place where animals roamed freely and the air smelled like wildflowers and fresh earth. There was something peaceful here. Timeless.

As I followed the path along the fence, letting my eyes roam over the quiet pasture, a sound rose above the stillness. Someone calling my name.

"Andi!"
I stopped. The voice was clear. Real. Not imagined.

I turned towardthe sound, heart racing now, and that's when I saw her.

Rachel.
My cousin.
Standing just on the other side of the fence, smiling like she always had, wide, warm, and unshaken by time.

My feet moved before I realized I was running. I reached her and threw my arms around her. Her embrace was exactly as I remembered, solid, comforting, alive. It didn't make sense, and yet it made perfect sense all at once. Tears welled up in my eyes.

"I can't believe it's really you," I whispered.

She nodded gently.

"It's me, Andi. I've been waiting for you."

I held her hand over the fence and told her how much I missed her, how the whole family missed her. I reminded her of how loved she was, how unfair it felt when ovarian cancer took her in her early fifties, how her daughter, Amber, still speaks of her with such longing.

Rachel's eyes softened.

"I know," she said gently. "But I'm at peace here. It's never lonely, and it's never boring. I'm with the ones who crossed over before us. There's laughter, music, work to do, and joy in everything. I'm whole again, Andi. The pain," she touched her lower abdomen gently, "it's all gone. My body had grown too tired. It couldn't carry my soul anymore. It was time."

I nodded, blinking back tears. Just standing with her, hearing her voice again, healed something in me I hadn't realized was still broken.

But then her tone deepened, edged with something new. "I know your time here is winding down," she said. "The next part of your journey is waiting. But before you go, I need to ask you something."

"Anything," I said quickly.

She took a deep breath, as her voice trembled with emotion. "Please tell Amber, my precious baby, that I love her with all my heart. Tell her that those moments when her heart skips, or my scent lingers around her, or she hears me in her dreams, she's not imagining it. It's me. I'm there."

I took her hand in mine and held it firmly. "I will, Rachel. I promise. I'll tell her everything."

"Good," she said with a relieved smile. "She needs

to know. She still hurts."

I hesitated a moment, then asked softly, "Rachel, have you seen my grandmother? I want to see her. I miss her so much."

Rachel's face lit up.
"Of course. She's waiting for you.
Follow the fence line a little further down. You'll see her. She's been watching for you since your arrival."

Tears filled my eyes and rolled down my cheeks. My grandmother had passed when I was little, but the thought of being reunited with her filled me with joy so strong it almost hurt. We had lived in the same house, and most nights I slept beside her. Losing her was one of the first deep wounds my soul had ever known.

I turned back to Rachel and pulled her into one last hug, our fingers linking through the fence slats.

"I love you," I whispered.

She smiled.

"I love you too. But Andi, don't forget to tell Amber. You know how forgetful you can be sometimes."

I laughed gently through the tears.
"I won't forget. I promise."

She watched me as I walked away, her voice drifting through the breeze one last time.

"Please don't forget. Not this."
I paused and turned back, lifting my hand in a final wave, holding her eyes for a lingering moment before continuing on.

I didn't know what waited beyond the next turn, but I knew who was calling me onward, and that knowing wrapped me in a calm I couldn't explain.

Chapter 10:
A Love That Never Left

As the fence line continued beside me, that calm shifted into a slow-building current, drawing me forward. The air changed first, growing dense and humming with something sacred. My heart began to flutter in quiet agreement. I didn't know where my feet were taking me, but I trusted the pull completely.

Up ahead, the path curved, and through a haze of golden sunlight, I saw it. First a shimmer, then shapes, then a massive, swelling crowd. A sea of people, countless as grains of sand, stretched as far as my eyes could see. It looked like some kind of grand event or gathering, but unlike anything earthly.

There was music in the air. But not from

instruments, the music was rising all around from my surroundings. The flowers seemed to sing in soft, fragrant tones. The grass whispered beneath my feet with a soothing hum. The trees swayed gently, their leaves rustling in rhythm like a classical chorus, while birds joined in with joyful clarity. It felt as if everything around me had awakened in perfect harmony, each part of creation lending its voice to a sacred symphony. As my soul leaned in, the music created a sense of euphoria. It stirred something sacred within me, pure, radiant, and full of welcome.

I pressed on and soon saw a crowd gathered around what appeared to be a colossal, radiant stadium. Seats were made of polished marble, and pillars were carved with symbols that pulsed with light. Every person there seemed to glow faintly, and yet none of them seemed unfamiliar. Somehow, I felt as if I knew them in spirit.

I approached a man near the edge of the crowd and said, almost in a whisper, "I'm looking for my grandmother. I don't know how to find her in the crowd of all of these people."

The man turned and, without hesitation, smiled. "Andi," he said, his voice as warm as fire on a winter night. "She's expecting you."

The instant the words left his mouth, something miraculous happened. People moved aside, parting like the sea for a ship cutting through its waters, forming a clear path through the center. The air itself felt as though it stopped moving the instant I saw her.

She was running toward me. Not walking. Not gliding. Running, just like she did when I was a child with skinned-knees and tear-streaked cheeks, needing only her arms to feel whole again. Her arms were wide open, and her smile lit up brighter than anything I'd ever seen. She came at me like a fullback powering up the middle of the field, unstoppable and fierce with love.

I broke into a sprint, tears already spilling down my cheeks. When we collided, I fell into her arms, and every crack in my heart, every ache that had lingered since she left my world, was suddenly and miraculously mended.

I instantly felt whole again. She smelled like lavender and Oil of Olay soap, just like I remembered. And when she cupped my face in her hands and softly patted my cheeks, I sobbed even harder.

"My Puddin'," she said, calling me by the nickname she'd given me as a toddler. The one that stuck all these years because of the way my chubby cheeks used to jiggle like pudding when I ran around. Only my close family ever called me that, and just hearing it again cracked me wide open, like a dam giving way under the weight of memory and love too long held back.

"I miss you every day," I choked. "I cry for you still. Sometimes it hurts so bad, just missing you."

She didn't respond right away. She just looked at me, eyes full of knowing, and brushed the tears from my face with both hands. "I know, baby. I know you do," she said softly. "But I'm here. I've always been with you."

Chapter 11:
Love Across Frequencies

A tide of questions rose before I could stop them. "But why haven't you come back to me? Why couldn't I see you before now?" I asked, desperately.

She gave me a gentle smile, her eyes bright with that quiet, soulful depth that always seemed to reach right into me.

"Remember, I am always with you," she said softly. "You'll feel my presence most when your spirit is at rest, during sleep or stillness, Puddin'. That's when your soul is free enough to meet with mine. You might not remember every dream, but I'm always there, keeping an eye on you, making sure you're okay, speaking to your spirit when the world grows quiet."

She paused, then said, "It's like radio stations, Puddin'. Each station has its own frequency. You can't hear two at once. The living and the spirit world operate much like different radio stations."

I nodded slowly. "I understand," I said, amazed that it all made sense now. "We're on different frequencies."

She leaned in, her quiet smile warming the air between us. "You're never alone," she whispered. "I know you've been struggling. I know you feel lonely sometimes, especially now that you're on your own again. But when you sleep, I curl up beside you, just so you won't feel so alone."

I broke down again. My shoulders were shaking. "I thought I imagined that, Grandma! I thought it was just my mind playing tricks on me."

"No, baby. It's just me."

I then told her about the strange experience earlier

in the day, the unsettling encounter in the tomato grove. I described the towering plants, the two silent farmers in overalls whose faces had turned purple, and how disturbed I'd been by their silence when I tried to speak to them.

"It scared me," I whispered. "I didn't know what to make of it."

She laughed, a light and sweet sound, like wind chimes dancing in a gentle breeze.
"You met angels, Puddin'. They weren't there to chit-chat. They had a task to fulfill. Their mission wasn't to ease your curiosity, but to deliver something important."

I looked at her, puzzled.

"They gave me two tomato plants and told me to plant them when I got home."

She nodded knowingly.
"And that purple you saw on their faces? That color was shown to you, so you'd understand. They're set apart from the other souls here. Marked. Chosen

for divine assignments."

She nodded again, her eyes full of pride.
"I know you didn't think much of those plants at first, but they matter. Those plants are symbols of God's provision. You've been praying for help, for relief. Puddin', there is no lack here. No shortage. No poverty. You were guided to that grove so you could witness divine abundance with your own eyes. And God will provide for you and your children. When you return home, the struggle you feel around money will begin to lift."

Tears of gratitude streamed down my face. "It's been so hard, Grandma. Since the divorce, I didn't know if I had the strength to keep going. Most days, it felt like I was barely holding myself together."

She held me close and whispered, "That season is over now, Puddin'. You've walked through the fire, but it didn't consume you. You're crossing into a new chapter of your life."

She gently pulled away and looked into my eyes. "We don't have much longer. The limo driver will be here soon to take you back."

I lowered my gaze to my watch, finding the time sitting at 5:55 PM.

I grabbed my grandmother tightly and held her in a long, lingering embrace, one that carried the weight of a lifetime and the warmth of home. Her arms wrapped around me with the same familiar strength I remembered from childhood, soft and sure, as if she could shield me from anything. I breathed in her scent, lavender and Oil of Olay, the scent of safety and unconditional love.

Her skin was warm, soft, and smooth against mine, and her touch radiated a peace that settled deep in my bones. I clung to her, not wanting to let go, hoping that if I held on tight enough, time might pause for us. She held me just as firmly, her hands gently patting my back, full of knowing and grace.

It was our final hug, yet it carried the echo of every embrace we had ever shared and the quiet promise that love like hers never truly leaves.

As I stepped away, she began to shine, her entire form blazing with a light so intense it stung my eyes. A quiet peace radiated from her like warmth from a fire.

I started walking, and her voice drifted towards me, warm as ever. "Don't forget to plant the tomatoes, Puddin'. And remember, I'm always with you."

The sea of people, my grandmother among them, began to fade behind me. Their forms slowly merged with the golden light until all that remained was a soft glow. A deep, steady peace settled over me, as if questions I had carried for years had quietly been answered. It wrapped around me like warm air. Yet even with that peace, my heart ached at the thought of leaving Celestial City behind.

I continued forward with steps so light they barely touched the ground, drifting toward the glowing archway marked Exit. Though my time there was ending, a quiet assurance rose within me, whispering that this wasn't a true goodbye, only an *I'll see you again.*

The moment I crossed the threshold, everything changed. The light dimmed, the colors drained, and the world around me dissolved from vivid brilliance into muted, lifeless shades. It felt like stepping from a vibrant color tv screen into an old black-and-white set. The warmth I'd carried from Celestial City gently slipped away, replaced by a stillness that settled deep in my chest. Not cold, just empty.

And there, waiting just as he promised, was the sleek black limo, its glossy surface reflecting the soft light from the City's gates. Leaning casually against the open driver's door was the same man who had greeted me at the very beginning.

He straightened up when he saw me approaching, his grin stretching wide across his face, like he already knew everything I was about to say.

"Well?" he called out, folding his arms, his voice filled with a knowing warmth. "How was your tour?"

I could only shake my head at first, still caught

between the realms of the divine and the earthly. "There are no words," I finally managed, my voice hoarse with emotion. "It was beyond amazing. It was magical. Sacred."

His eyes crinkled at the corners as he opened the back door of the limo with a graceful sweep.

"I told you," he said softly, with the kind of certainty that left no room for doubt.

I paused before stepping inside, meeting his eyes. "You were right," I said, my voice trembling slightly. "It wasn't just a tour. Every single detail was tailored for me."

The driver chuckled as I slid into the back seat, his laughter low and knowing, like he'd heard stories like mine before. His laughter steadied me, reminding me that in my life there is still so much to anticipate and appreciate.

Chapter 12:
A New Woman

As we pulled away from the exit gates, the City behind us faded into a soft, golden blur. I began to recount it all: every moment, every revelation. I spoke of the angels with violet-tinted faces, the Corridor of Reunion, the sea of souls that parted like a miracle, and the long-awaited embrace with my grandmother that mended something deep inside me.

He never interrupted. He just drove, hands steady on the wheel, eyes occasionally flicking up to the rearview mirror to meet mine. He nodded, smiled, and sometimes let out a soft "Mmm," as if he were savoring every word like a song he hadn't heard before.

I spoke freely, with a calm clarity that surprised even me.

Time felt suspended, stretched thin between the place I'd just left and the one waiting ahead. It was only when the limo slowed and turned onto a long gravel road that I realized we had arrived. The Caverns of Hades Hollow loomed in the distance, dark and imposing. The limo crept to a halt at the designated pickup spot, where the cavern's dim lights flickered against the dust-filled air.

Just beyond the exit archway, I spotted them. My friends stood huddled together like survivors of something unspeakable. They looked worn out and furious, as if they'd just come back from a battle they never signed up for. Their clothes were torn and dirty, their makeup smeared by sweat and tears. The look in their eyes told me everything.

Alexis stood rigid, arms crossed and jaw clenched. Chyna paced in tight, furious circles, muttering under her breath. Morgan, missing a shoe, stood glaring back at the path as if daring it to come at her again.

The driver's gaze followed mine as he brought the car to a stop. He let out a low whistle and said, "Wow! It looks like your friends have gone through a terrible ordeal."

Then, with a glance back at me, his tone softened. "But you, you're not the same woman I dropped off."

I met his eyes in the mirror, feeling the truth of his words settle warmly in my chest. I smiled, hand resting on the door handle.

"No," I whispered. "I'm not."

Chapter 13:
To Hell and Back

———— ◇ ————

With that, the moment between us gently passed. The driver, still wearing that same calm smile he always had, stepped out and swung open the door for my friends to climb in. The poor man didn't know what kind of storm he was about to unleash inside his car.

Alexis wasted no time. She practically threw herself into the back seat, flopping down dramatically, and blurted out, "That was the worst tour ever! I am never setting foot in that God-forsaken place again!
Look at us!
Our clothes are ruined.
Ruined!"

She gestured wildly at her destroyed designer outfit and cried out, "These clothes were supposed to see the Eiffel Tower, not the inside of Satan's basement!"

She didn't even take a breath before launching into the next grievance. "It was so filthy! And the cave passages? So narrow, we were practically stacked on top of each other like a pile of dirty laundry! We were supposed to have a private tour, but nooo, the next thing you know, we're herded in with a bunch of sweaty strangers like cattle headed for slaughter! I cannot wait to get ahold of my travel agent. Oh, he's going to hear every bit of this. I'm going to tear his tail apart."

Before I could even blink, Morgan stumbled in behind her, eyes glassy with tears, limping dramatically like she'd just survived a major accident. She held up one bare foot for everyone to see, wailing, "I lost my Fendi boot!" She sniffled pitifully.

"It got swept away when that nasty cave water started pouring out of the rocks like some kind of horror movie! It just, it just took my boot!"

She plopped down next to Alexis, who was still mid-rant, both of them now trying to talk over each other in the grand tradition of best friends who have absolutely no intention of letting anyone else get a word in.

Then Chyna stormed in, fanning herself with both hands like she'd just escaped a house fire. "And don't even get me started on the heat!" she barked.

"It was like somebody cranked the thermostat up to the seventh circle of hell! I swear I almost fainted. I thought I was gonna die right there between a rock wall and some sweaty man named John."

She paused for dramatic effect, then gagged loudly.

"And the SMELL! Oh my LORD. The SMELL! It was like roadkill and rotten eggs had a baby and left it to marinate in that cave for six months!"

I tried, really tried, to look sympathetic. I even gave

them my best "Oh no, poor you" face. But inside, I was biting my lip to keep from laughing.

I finally chimed in, trying to soothe their wounded egos. "I'm so sorry, you guys. I really am. I feel awful that your tour was so terrible."

And honestly, I did feel bad. But let's be real. I knew they had set themselves up for disaster the minute they decided to tour muddy, slippery caverns dressed like they were about to strut the red carpet. Designer handbags, silk scarves, and four-inch stilettos to go spelunking? It just didn't make any sense. It was like sending a bunch of runway models into a mud wrestling match.

After a good fifteen minutes of venting, sighing, and general despair, the limo grew quiet enough for them to finally notice me.

It all kicked off when Alexis gave me one of her "I'm watching you" squints.

"Wait a minute," she said, cocking her head to the side. "Why do you look like you just came from a day spa? You're, you're glowing!"

Morgan and Chyna immediately joined in, staring at me like I was some rare specimen.

"Yeah," Chyna said.
"You look different. Peaceful. Happy."

At first, I hesitated. After everything they'd been through, it felt almost cruel to tell them how magical my experience had been. I mean, they looked like they'd clawed their way up from a sewer tunnel.

But it was bursting out of me. I just couldn't hold it in.

And so, all the way home, I told them. I recapped my Celestial City tour. I gave them every breathtaking corridor, every beautiful soul I'd encountered, every tiny detail that shimmered in my memory. I spoke with a freedom I hadn't felt in years.

In the past, I had always been the quiet one, the listener, the one who just sat back while they told their wild, outrageous stories about their adventures. My life had always been simple, quiet, nothing extravagant. I never really had anything extraordinary to add to the conversation.

But this time, I had the story that left them wide-eyed and hanging onto every word.

Time flew by faster than any of us realized. One moment we were gasping over my retelling, the next we were pulling into the familiar streets of home. The exhaustion from the day finally caught up with us, heavy and undeniable. But so did a strange, warm sense of togetherness. Like maybe the day hadn't been such a disaster after all.

The limo driver, who had listened with quiet amusement the whole way, began dropping us off one by one.

I was the first to go.
As I gathered my things, we all leaned in for a group hug, sweaty, smelly, dirt-streaked and all. We promised that we weren't going to let so much time pass between get-togethers anymore. We swore, right then and there, that we'd meet for lunch at

least once a month, no matter how busy life got.

And while it wasn't the day any of us had planned, somehow, between the laughter, the dirt, and the memories, it became a day none of us would ever forget.

Chapter 14:
When the Harvest Comes

————— ◇ —————

As I stepped inside the quiet house, the stillness wrapped around me like a soft blanket. For a moment, I just stood in the entryway, taking it all in: the silence, the peace. The kids were away for the night, staying at a friend's place, and for the first time in a while, the house was all mine. No noise, no demands. Just stillness.

I set my things down on the kitchen table, my fingers grazing over the smooth wood as I centered myself. That's when I noticed the tomato plants. The same ones the angel had placed in my hands, now shimmering softly in the fading light, almost glowing, as if gently reminding me to plant them. Without hesitating, I picked them up and stepped back outside.

Even though the sun had almost slipped completely behind the horizon and evening was settling into night, I was determined to get those plants into the ground. With a steady sense of purpose, I carried them to a small patch of earth just beyond the kitchen window. The sky was streaked in shades of pink and deep gold, the final light of day offering just enough light to guide my hands.

On my knees in the warm dirt, I dug carefully, reverently. I planted each tiny vine with my own hands, pressing the soil gently around their fragile stems. I whispered a prayer over them, not just a prayer for growth, but a prayer of remembrance. And now, every day when I look out that window, I will be reminded of God's provision, His quiet hand at work, guiding my steps and holding me steady, even when I cannot see the way.

I brushed the dirt from my hands and went back inside. Planting the seedlings felt complete: simple, yet deeply meaningful. I had just started to settle in when I remembered the mail.

I walked out to the curbside mailbox, the warm evening air brushing against my skin. The metal door creaked as I opened it and pulled out a small stack of envelopes. Bills, flyers, the usual clutter of everyday life. I headed back inside, sorting through them without much thought. Then I froze. One envelope stopped me cold. It was from my ex husband.

My first instinct was hesitation. Over the last year, any letters from him rarely brought anything good. But something nudged me forward, so I tore it open.

Inside was a check. Not just any check, but one covering every penny of the past-due child support he owed. And tucked behind it was another one, this time paying for the children's entire school tuition for the year.

The papers fluttered from my hands as I crumbled to the floor, sobs wrenching from deep within me. I knelt there, hands covering my face, tears pouring down my cheeks. I wept, not out of sadness, but out of sheer, overwhelming gratitude.

"Thank you, God," I whispered, over and over again. "Thank you for hearing me.
Thank you for changing what I thought was unchangeable."

For so long, I had prayed for a miracle. Not just for money, but for his heart to soften, for bitterness to give way to responsibility, for the impossible to happen. And now, here it was, sitting in my trembling hands.

But God wasn't finished yet.

In the weeks that followed, blessings unfolded so quickly they left me breathless. Out of nowhere, without warning and without so much as a formal interview, I was called into my manager's office.

I sat across from him, nerves dancing in my stomach, as he smiled and slid a crisp letter across the desk toward me.

"Congratulations," he said. "You've been promoted to Director of Loan Operations."

For a moment, I just stared at him, blinking in

disbelief. I hadn't even known I was being considered for the role. Yes, I had worked late nights. Yes, I had poured my heart into my job. But this was grace.

The promotion came with a sixty percent salary increase, a number so unreal I had to read it twice just to believe it. And that wasn't all. It included a company car, my own reserved parking spot, a generous retirement plan, and flexible hours. Benefits that meant I would no longer have to worry about putting food on the table, keeping my children clothed, or surviving the next unexpected crisis.

For the first time in years, I felt like I could breathe. Truly breathe. No more scrambling to make ends meet. No more sleepless nights wondering how I would stretch a dollar far enough. The weight I had carried for so long had finally lifted.

With that new sense of stability settling in, I opened a college savings account for the kids. Each child support payment and every unexpected blessing went straight into it, little by little building a future that had once felt impossibly out of reach.

In the days that followed, I found myself drawn to the kitchen window every morning. With a warm cup of coffee in hand and the soft light drifting across the room, I would look out at those tomato plants, now strong and reaching toward the sun. And each time, I whispered the same words my grandmother had spoken to me in Celestial City: *"God will provide for you and your children."*

And standing there, wrapped in the fullness of God's promise, I knew she had been right all along.

But the journey of confirmation wasn't over yet.

A few months later, at Christmas service, I spotted my cousin Amber at church. The sight of her made my heart thud with nerves as Rachel's request came rushing back, the message I had promised to deliver. I almost didn't do it, just wanting to keep it to myself. I was worried Amber would think I had lost my mind, standing there in the aisle with something so heavy and strange to say. But the words pressed against my heart, refusing to be silenced.

I walked up to her after service, took a deep breath, and said, "I know this might sound strange, but your mother sent a message through me. She told me to tell you that she loves you with all her heart. She said that in those moments when your heart skips, or her scent lingers around you, or you hear her in your dreams, you're not imagining it. It's her. She's there. She's with you."

The moment the words left my mouth, Amber burst into tears, full aching sobs as she wrapped her arms around me. Through her tears she managed to say, "I needed to hear that. More than you know. It's the best Christmas gift I could have ever asked for."

Tears filled my own eyes, and at that moment, I knew Rachel's message had found the heart it was meant to heal.

Still, another question tugged at me, one I had tucked away since Celestial City.

I had promised myself I would find out if what my great-grandmother Jane had told me was real. After weeks of wrestling with doubt, I finally ordered a DNA test. It felt strange and scary, like stepping across a bridge that could not be uncrossed.

When the results came back, the truth was undeniable.

I was not a McGuire by blood, but perhaps by divine design, I was meant to be part of their legacy.

It seemed that long ago, my great grandmother had separated from her husband and conceived my grandfather with another man. A story hidden in silence had finally come to light. But instead of shattering me, the truth settled like a soft, honest rain.

With the help of the DNA results, I traced my lineage back to Jane Polite, my great-grandmother. She was the one who had embraced me that day near the ocean, who had poured strength and knowing into me with a tenderness that still echoes in my soul.

It was all real.
It had all happened just as she said.

And somehow, knowing where I truly came from made me feel more whole, not less.

My roots had simply run deeper than I ever realized, woven through unseen hands that had been guiding me all along.

The truth settled into my spirit like rich soil around new roots, nurturing something I could not see, yet had always been there, quietly growing. Even the small shift in what I thought I knew about my family rose slowly, almost timidly, as if it knew I needed time to accept it.

With that unseen growth came a deeper awareness of God's provision. Not just in finances or newfound stability, but in gentler, quieter ways.

He restored the hope I thought I had lost.

He redeemed the parts of me that had been worn thin and broken, even the quiet places in me that had been hidden and were now being gently brought to light.

And in the soil of my life, where pain once lived, He planted something beautiful. Something lasting, something alive, something that stood firm and would continue to grow long after the turbulence in my life had quieted.

As I stood there, feeling the fullness of it all, a fierce certainty stirred deep within me.

This was not the end of my story. Nooo... I knew that with every part of me.

It was the beginning of a life I had once only dared to dream about. Rebuilt from brokenness, born from grace, and destined to bloom in ways I had yet to imagine.

The storm had passed.
The seeds had been planted.
And now, it was time to rise.

The End

www.ingramcontent.com/pod-product-compliance
Lightning Source LLC
Chambersburg PA
CBHW030346030726
47499CB00003B/927